This Walker book belongs to:

iS Amamar
....

....

....

To you, Finn and Sawyer –
in homage to your wondrous, marvellous
and glorious imaginations!

First published 2014 by Walker Books Ltd, 87 Vauxhall Walk, London SE11 5HJ • This edition published 2015 • © 2014 Timothy Basil Ering • The right of Timothy Basil Ering to be identified as author/illustrator of this work has been asserted by him in accordance with the Copyright, Designs and Patents Act 1988 • This book has been typeset in Wilke Bold • Printed in China • All rights reserved. No part of this book may be reproduced, transmitted or stored in an information retrieval system in any form or by any means, graphic, electronic or mechanical, including photocopying, taping and recording, without prior written permission from the publisher. • British Library Cataloguing in Publication Data: a catalogue record for this book is available from the British Library • ISBN 978-1-4063-6068-4 • www.walker.co.uk • 10 9 8 7 6 5 4 3 2 1

The Almost Fearless Hamilton Squidlegger

TIMOTHY BASIL ERING

WALKER BOOKS
AND SUBSIDIARIES
LONDON · BOSTON · SYDNEY · AUCKLAND

During the hours when the sun shares its light, Hamilton is a daring do-*er* and a dream-come-true*r*. Why, he's the rippingest, roaringest Squidlegger in the scrintalberry swamp!

"Dad! Dad! Watch, Dad!" Hamilton calls out. "My mighty shield can block the flames of a fire-breathing frackensnapper!"

"Amazing, Hamilton! Your strength and speed are stupendous," says Dad.

"And my sword can dodge the claws of a skelecragon!"

"What courage you have! It takes one brave Squidlegger to tickle the foot of a bracklesneed!"

One might say Hamilton Squidlegger is fearless.
Well, not quite. He's *almost* fearless...

You see, when the sun disappears behind the scrintalberry trees, it won't be long before it's ...

Each night at bedtime, Hamilton's dad has to plead with Hamilton. "Please, please, *pleeeeeeeease*, son – stay in your own mud tonight," he says.

All alone, Hamilton lasts about two minutes before he hears something. *What's that?*

Is it the sound of a frackensnapper? Or a skelecragon? Or a bracklesneed?

Hamilton springs from his mud ...

and scrambles to his secret hideaway!

The next day, when the sun snaps up from behind
the scrintalberry trees, Hamilton wakes with vigour.
He is fearless once again!

Well, friends, this went on until one particular afternoon when Hamilton was sneaking,

wrestling

and sword fighting,

his nose discovered the scent of something that dreams are made of...

A double-decker grasshopper worm-cake, with snake-belly frosting! It was Hamilton's absolute favourite treat.

"I made this especially for you, Hamilton," said his father. "You can eat it *all* for breakfast tomorrow, on one condition: tonight, you must *stay in your own mud*."

"Anything! Anything for that delicious cake!" Hamilton exclaimed.

But when steel-grey rain clouds darkened the swamp
and the *BOOM* of thunder shook the scrintalberries,
Hamilton had doubts.

"What if a l-l-lightning monster comes tonight?" he asked, crawling reluctantly into his mud.

"Ha!" scoffed his dad. "What if one does? Think good thoughts is what I say. Monsters are silly, and they love to play! Have a cake fight with it." He gave Hamilton a kiss good night, gently patted him between the eyes, then doused the light.

Hamilton knew he would be too afraid to have
a cake fight with any lightning monster.

Plus he wanted to *eat* the cake – *yawn!* –
not play with it.

He imagined
licking the
delicious
frosting...

He imagined the yummy crunch
of the baked grasshoppers...

He was a
tongue-length away
from a juicy,
soft-boiled
worm,
when ...

SPLAT! There was a lightning monster!
And his dad was right behind it, throwing a glop of
cake at the monster's ear! Grasshoppers and worms
splattered everywhere as the monster scraped off some
snake-belly frosting and hurled it right back.

Off they ran, giggling and laughing, till they were out
of sight. Hamilton followed the trail of frosting.

When the trail ended at an old TV, Hamilton
turned and twisted the knobs. "Where are you, Dad?"
At that very moment, he heard his dad's voice,
and appearing in the TV screen, pedalling a triple-seated
skragencycle, were his dad and the lightning monster.
"Nothing to be afraid of, son, is what I say. Monsters come
because they want to play!"

Then the TV shook wildly as though it were alive, and out from the top, bottom and sides, a bracklesneed's tentacles appeared and grew bigger and bigger! What's more, the TV was squirting and spraying hundreds of gallons of pink lemonade *everywhere*!

Soon the entire place was flooded. Luckily, Hamilton
was able to climb aboard a passing ship. But unluckily,
the bracklesneed wanted to board the ship too!

The ship's bow heaved in the huge pink waves, tossing Hamilton through the air and right down through a hatch into the galley, where a striped bass stood calmly at a stove, humming sea shanties and cooking pancakes.

"A monster is trying to sink the ship!" Hamilton screamed. "No worries, mate!" the bass replied. "I've invited it for a snack. Always be nice to a bracklesneed is what I say. They make great friends, and they love to play." And the fish asked Hamilton to help the bracklesneed into the galley.

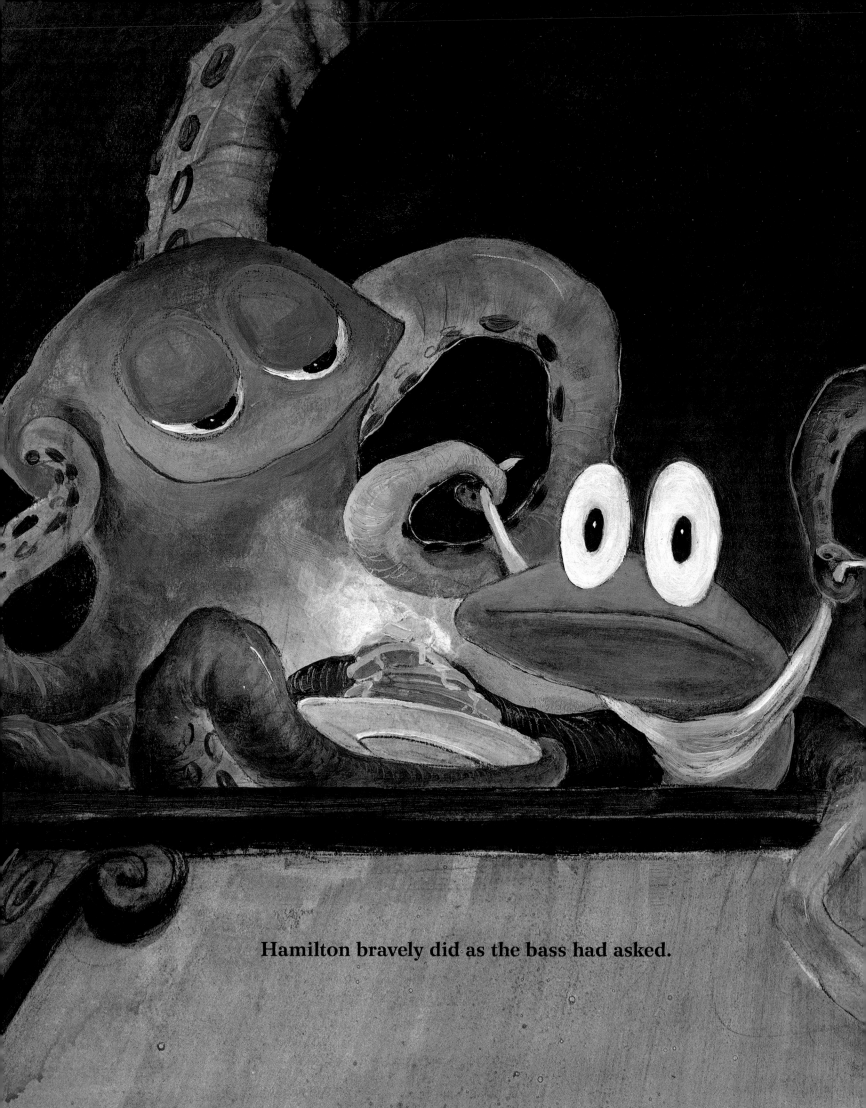

Hamilton bravely did as the bass had asked.

"Now to feed my other two friends," the fish
said, flipping some pancakes up through the hatch.
"Upward ho!" he shouted.

Hamilton climbed up and was amazed to see that
the skelecragon was now manning the helm. The
frackensnapper was on board too!

"Trim the balloon rigging," cried the bass while he and
the bracklesneed mounted the deck. "Upward ho, we go!"

Powered by the frackensnapper's wild breath, the ship
began to rise. They sailed through the air ...

over magnificent and breathtaking things.

But Hamilton missed his dad.

Hamilton borrowed a spotting scope and looked far and wide. Following a rainbow all the way down to where its arc began, he saw something that made his eyes widen with joy.

"Dad!" cried Hamilton. "Dad! Dad!"

Who should be on that cloud but his beloved dad and the lightning monster! The ship raced down the arc, and everyone was thrilled to be reunited.

A celebration ensued, and oh, my, could those Squidleggers dance! The friends played and sang together until …

the sun began to slip down behind the horizon. Hamilton
climbed back up to the poop deck and gazed out. He knew
he needed to tell the others before it got too late...

"It's bedtime!" Hamilton proclaimed.

All the friends cheered with joy!

They hurried off to brush their teeth and wash their faces, hands, claws and tentacles so that they could listen to Hamilton's dad read them a book before they all went to sleep …

in their very own cabins.

And that was the moment when the *almost* fearless
Hamilton Squidlegger became *totally* fearless.

The End